D0478180

For Frankie, Billy and Ged
~ A G

For Grandma and Grandpa
Scarborough, with love
~ C W

LITTLE TIGER PRESS
1 The Coda Centre, 189 Munster Road, London SW6 6AW
www.littletigerpress.com
First published in Great Britain 2001
This edition published 2012
by Little Tiger Press, London
Text copyright © Adèle Geras 2001
Illustrations copyright © Catherine Walters 2001
Adèle Geras and Catherine Walters have asserted their
rights to be identified as the author and illustrator of this
work under the Copyright, Designs and Patents Act, 1988
All rights reserved • ISBN 978-1-85430-725-5
Printed in China • LTP/1900/0456/0512
2 4 6 8 10 9 7 5 3 1

SLEEP TIGHT, GINGER KITTEN

Adèle Geras

Catherine Walters

LITTLE TIGER PRESS

A ginger kitten
with one white paw,
and a small white
spot on his ginger
face is looking for
a sleeping place …

The ginger kitten
likes to leap
and jump
and run
and sit
and creep.

But best of all
he likes to sleep.

The ginger kitten
finds a chair.
It's made of wood,
and much too hard
for his furry feet.
He can't sleep there.

The ginger kitten
lies on the floor
in the bathroom
behind the door.

He licks a paw
and washes his nose,
and when he's clean ...

...he snuggles into the
kitten-shaped space.
Then someone opens
the bathroom door
and pushes it into
his sleepy face.
The spot isn't comfy
anymore.
So out he dashes
across the floor!

The ginger kitten
sees a box.
Inside the box
it's smelly and dark
and much too small . . .

...so the kitten creeps out.
He looks about ...

and then he finds
the mat in the hall.

He stretches out
his two front paws
and *abracadabra*,
there are his claws!
Scritch! Scratch!
He scratches the mat.
The ginger kitten
loves doing that.

He goes upstairs
and jumps on a bed ...

but somebody comes and disturbs his play.
No soft beds for this kitten today!

The ginger kitten
sees that the door
of the wardrobe is
open so in he goes.
He bumps his head
on the hanging clothes.
The floor is covered
with pairs of shoes.
This isn't a place where
the kitten can snooze!

The ginger kitten runs downstairs, and
pushes the door of the lounge with his nose.
He tiptoes in on velvety paws …

There's a child on the sofa,
a child he knows.

The ginger kitten
jumps up and purrs
and curls up there on
the child's warm lap.
He's found the perfect
place for a nap!